ESCAPE FROM VICTORY

A DUBLIN TRILOGY NOVELLA

CAIMH MCDONNELL

Copyright © 2023 by McFori Ink

All rights reserved.

No part of this book may be reproduced in any form or by any electronic or mechanical means including information storage and retrieval systems, without permission in writing from the author. The only exception is by a reviewer, who may quote short excerpts in a review.

This book is a work of fiction. Names, characters, places, and incidents either are products of the author's imagination or are used fictitiously. Any resemblance to actual persons, living or dead, events, or locales is entirely coincidental.

Caimh McDonnell

Visit my website at www.WhiteHairedirishman.com

First edition: March 2023

ISBN: 978-1-912897-54-4

AUTHOR'S NOTE

Dear Reader,

I'm going to be honest with you – I have a problem. Previously, I tried to write a Bunny McGarry novella, and it ended up becoming a full novel. This time, I tried to write a short story, and it ended up morphing into a novella. Worse than that, the aforementioned exists in the world of the Dublin Trilogy, a series which now contains seven novels and counting. This means we get angry e-mails every week from people who can not only count, but who take that counting stuff seriously. What makes all of this so much more maddening is that the problem is only getting worse. I'd already had an idea for the eighth book in the infuriatingly titled series and while writing this no-longer-a-short-story novella, I had the idea for a ninth novel involving some of these characters which I'm now going to have to write.

As an incredibly lazy person, you have no idea how upsetting this is for me. I start these projects with the best of intentions and then, well, Bunny gets behind the wheel (literally in the case of this) and all bets are off. The root of the issue seems to be that not only does he live in my head 24/7, but he has no end of adventures he would like to tell me about. Outside of the Dublin Trilogy, Bunny is mad keen to tell me what is happening in the McGarry Stateside series, so the fourth instalment of that will be coming later this year.

So, this is a novella – which, in case you're wondering, is longer than a short story and shorter than a novel. As novellas go, this is a short one, but it still qualifies and, more importantly, the tier between short story and novella is called novelette and I'm refusing to write one of them as it sounds way too much like a sanitary product.

Regardless, I hope you enjoy it as, whether or not either of us like it, I fear Bunny McGarry has a lot more tales to tell.

Happy Reading!

Caimh

CHAPTER ONE

Bunny McGarry looked around the corner of the supermarket car park where the St Jude's Under-12s hurling team had gathered. He was unsure what the collective noun for a group of pre-teen boys was – a slouch? A bedragglement? An exhaustion? Regardless, it was a statistically proven fact that if you left eighteen of them to their own devices for more than three minutes, one of them would inevitably carry out a minor act of violence on another.

"Donnacha Aherne," snapped Bunny. "Did I just see you giving Johnny Marsh a dead arm?"

"No, Bunny," responded the perpetrator. "There's no way you could've seen me do that from where you are."

"I didn't. But I heard Johnny scream out in pain."

It tells you all you need to know about the workings of the male mind that after this statement; the puncher gave the punchee a look that had an unmistakable air of betrayal which, in turn, was met with an apologetic grimace from his victim.

"It seems to have slipped your attention, Donnacha, that we have a game this morning and, crazy as this may seem, I think it will be tactically sound if all of our players turned up in one piece."

"To be fair, boss, you did say last week that Johnny would be a better hurler if he only had the one arm." This interjection came from the only non-player amongst the eighteen, the St Jude's assistant manager, one Deccie Fadden.

Bunny glared down at him. "Thank you, Declan. As always, your seeming inability to grasp basic sarcasm is invaluable."

"You're welcome, boss."

Bunny shook his head and handed Deccie the plastic bag full of his purchases. "Here, replenishments for the first-aid kit." Plasters, oranges and a new magic sponge. He'd splashed out, as today was a big game.

Deccie looked into the bag and then looked back up at Bunny. "Where's the can of Coke and two Chomps you said you were getting me?"

This was met with a blank expression.

"Let me guess – that was more of that sarcasm stuff again, wasn't it?"

"See, you're slowly getting the hang of it, Deccie."

"Have you never heard the expression, boss, that sarcasm is the lowest form of wit? Oscar Wilde said that."

Bunny raised an eyebrow. Declan Fadden was full of surprises. "To be fair to old Oscar Wilde, he'd not seen you on the trip home from last week's match doing your recital of all the different fart noises you can make."

"Say what you like," said Deccie, with no small amount of pride, "that absolutely killed."

"It did." Loath as he was to admit it, it had been that funny, Bunny had been forced to pull the minibus over for fear of a traffic accident.

He clapped his hands together. "Right, lads, form a line."

"Actually," said Jason Phillips, "we're already in a line."

Bunny, like every other person in authority, found Jason Phillips alarming. A slight-built skinny kid, who wore thick jam jar glasses and looked like he could blow himself into orbit if he sneezed too vigorously. He also gave off the disconcerting impression of being smarter than everybody else in the room. In fact, quite possibly, that he was smarter than everybody else full stop. What made it worse was he clearly wasn't trying to give off that notion, it was just the way he was. He would be staring off into the distance one minute and then absentmindedly say something the next that you would spend several weeks thinking about. His comments had prompted Bunny to make trips to the library twice in the last three months to try to understand what he said. One of the times he'd wanted to check that Jason's explanation of how black holes worked tallied with what popular science knew already, because if it didn't, he thought they might have to tell somebody. The kid was *that* smart. The fact that he'd come up with it during a training session, when Bunny had been attempting to get the lads to string a few passes together, had been even more perplexing.

Several of the boys assembled in that particular corner of that particular supermarket car park were considered nightmares to teach, but Jason was the only one who actually kept teachers up at night. His was the kind of mind that needed to be properly nurtured, because it could go on to do truly great things. In this regard, it was quite like a big old chunk of enriched uranium. All kids had potential, but his was truly world-changing, in either direction.

Bunny knew how the teachers felt. He worried about putting Jason out on a hurling field in case a flailing stick caught him a glancing blow and cost the world a cure for cancer or the secrets to interstellar space flight, or at the very least, an explanation as to how every call centre is always experiencing higher than average call volumes. He always made sure Jason was wearing one of the team's three fancy new helmets with extra padding and the enormous bars on the front. A few weeks ago, Bunny had asked Jason why he had joined the hurling team and his response had been that he enjoyed the angles. The kid said stuff like that all the time, and nobody could tell if he was joking or not.

Following a disintegrating domestic situation, Jason now lived with his widowed uncle, John-Joe, who dug ditches for the council. Heaven knows what sort of conversations they had over dinner, but the lad appeared to be content enough and was certainly a lot safer than he had been. Bunny knew John-Joe a little; a relaxed, amiable fella, he seemed happy enough to let Jason be Jason while doing all he could to support him. That was a big improvement on what had gone before. Jason's mother had long since disappeared and his father was an abusive alcoholic who was in and out of rehab. The cumulative effect of all this on Jason was hard to read but worrying. How those parents had produced a genius was anybody's guess, and quite probably worthy of serious study.

Last year, after the results of a test given to every kid in Ireland came back, Jason had been offered a full scholarship to attend Belvedere College. To the surprise of everyone involved, he had politely turned it down by explaining that he did not believe in the concept of a private education. Nobody had been able to convince him otherwise. Bunny had even tried to have a word, but the lad had calmly explained that all he needed was a library card, pen and paper. That was the thing – beneath the pre-teen bumbling professor persona, lay something hard and unrelenting. Same as when an opposition player had taken Padraig Brooke out with a horrendous tackle a few weeks ago. Jason, who had shown minimal interest in the game until that point, had needed to be held back from exacting violent vengeance on the perpetrator, a rage bubbling up that was only tangentially related to a teammate getting smashed across the kneecaps. You saw it a lot in kids coming from situations like his, but it didn't make it any less dangerous or easier to cope with. Jason worried everyone because he seemed to be casually sauntering down the line between success story and cautionary tale, and nobody was sure which way things might fall.

Speaking of lines, for all of Jason's undoubted smarts, Bunny knew what a line was, and he was damn sure that the lads were not currently forming one. "With all due respect, Jason, the boys are not in a line."

"Actually," said Jason, not looking up from staring at a spiderweb crack in the concrete, "if we take us to be seventeen individual points, then it is possible to form an infinite array of lines between us."

Everyone in attendance went quiet and looked at each other for a few seconds. This happened a lot around Jason. The silence was broken by the boy himself. "What you mean, Bunny, is that you would like us to form a straight line."

Bunny nodded furiously. "OK, yes – right you are. Form a straight line please, lads." He leaned in towards Jason. "Thanks for the clarification."

Jason nodded and smiled without a hint of malice. "Of course, this assumes we're talking in only three dimensions."

"Let's assume we are," said Bunny quickly, looking at his watch. "We need to be getting a move on."

"But Phil isn't here yet," said Deccie.

"Phil isn't coming."

Deccie's face was a picture of shock. "What are ye on about? Phil Nellis never misses a game. He might be a waste of space, but he's a reliable waste of space."

"Yeah," agreed Bunny, "I've spent the last ten minutes on the phone explaining that to one of my colleagues. Do you remember that shed in Phil's garden?"

"His lab? Course."

"Well, hang onto that memory because it isn't there anymore. It blew up last night."

"How did that happen?"

"Apparently, Phil has narrowed it down to three possible sources. He'll have plenty of time to figure it out. Sounds like he's grounded until he turns eighty."

"Harsh."

"Well, his aunt and uncle aren't over-the-moon about

the fire brigade and the gardaí rolling up at 6am on a Sunday morning."

"The cops?" asked Deccie. "Why would they care?"

"Because, while we are in a time of blessed peace on this tortured isle, things blowing up is still something the gardaí take a significant interest in." The part Bunny left out was that Phil's uncle Paddy was popularly believed to be a high-end thief par excellence, one that, bar one early stumble, kept himself so far ahead of law enforcement that he was probably lapping them by now. The incident offered the local constabulary a free go at tearing their house apart and generally going on a fishing expedition. Nobody expected to find anything, Paddy was too smart for that, but they would enjoy inconveniencing him as much as possible. Bunny's assertion that the explosion was invariably the result of a certain curious kid's curious mind had not been greeted enthusiastically by the DI in charge. Still, it happened to be true. As was the fact that they'd lost a player they could ill-afford to. Phil Nellis was useless, but his willingness to stand in front of anyone, or anything, while being so, made him a useful form of useless. If all else failed, the kid would have a bright career as a speedbump.

"Inspection!" said Bunny, clapping his hands together.

The lads had now formed what even Jason would struggle to define as a straight line.

The inspection phase of proceedings, while it looked to the casual observer like a middle-aged man living out his tragic military fantasies, was actually a crucial part of the pre-game process. Bunny had learned this through bitter experience.

"Present ... arms!"

The boys duly held their football boots out in one hand and their shorts out in the other. Bunny took care of washing the jerseys and there was a large pile of hurling sticks and helmets alongside them in the storage compartment on the top of the minibus, but shorts and boots were the responsibility of the individual. He carried a couple of spares, but he still needed the majority of the team to remember their kit. Besides, at least one of the spare pairs of shorts now had so many holes in it that it technically qualified as lingerie. He walked up the line, Deccie falling in to step beside him. "Colm, clean your studs. Johnny, either wash those shorts for next week or take them out and shoot them before they run off on their own. Wayne O'Brien ..." Bunny stopped to take in the magnificent awfulness of what was presented before him. "Right, lads, my position on bullying is well known to all of you. What diabolic dipshit did this to poor Wayne's boots?"

"I did," said Wayne, cheerfully.

Bunny took one of the two offending boots out of Wayne's hands. It was luminous yellow. "What?"

"I used a highlighter to make them yellow."

"Why?"

"Y'know – so I'd stand out."

Bunny hesitated. He was resisting the urge to point out that if Wayne wanted to stand out, managing to make contact with the ball rather than taking divots out of the ground as he swung his hurling stick around like a man who had a grudge against the earth would be a great start. He didn't say that though, as he'd been working on trying to be positive. The team was on an eight-game losing streak and he'd got a book from the library on man management that had been only marginally less confusing than the one on black holes. He'd only read the first three chapters, but he had found himself wholeheartedly agreeing with whoever had written '*this is all bollix*' in the margin of page fifty-seven. Still, Butch had suggested he try positivity, and, for at least this week, he was going to give it a damn good go. With this in mind, Bunny took a deep breath and went with, "What on earth possessed you to do that to your boots?"

"One of them footballers on *Match of the Day* had it."

This was met with a collective wince from the group. Bunny's attitude to soccer was well known by everyone. Or at least everyone who wasn't Wayne O'Brien. The kid wasn't stupid, he just had a perpetually sunny, damn-near-oblivious outlook on life that from a distance looked an awful lot like stupid. Stupid tripped over a tiger because it wasn't paying attention to where it was going. Wayne walked over to nudge it with his foot because he wanted to make friends. Much to the annoyance of more careful souls, this approach to life, against all probability and logical sense, worked for Wayne. Even now, he was beaming up at Bunny with the light-hearted certainty that nothing bad could possibly happen. You couldn't dislike Wayne, and several people had tried.

"Right, well, it's against regulations."

"What regulations?" asked Wayne.

Before Bunny could respond, Deccie stepped forward until he was inches from Wayne's face. "Are you giving cheek, sonny Jim, m'lad? You'll be running laps of the car park faster than lasagne through a donkey. You mark my words. I'll make you wish you'd—"

Deccie was interrupted by Bunny pulling him back. "All right, Sergeant Slaughter, dial it back a few notches."

"We can't have dissent in the ranks, boss. Not today, of all days."

"Today is just another match," said Bunny, the hint of warning in his voice going so far over Deccie's head that it was a danger to commercial air traffic.

"No, it's not boss. It's the shower of Southsiders from Saint Mungo's, the one's managed by that DI Grainger, the guard you said was your nemesis …"

"We don't need to—" started Bunny, in a vain effort to stop the high-speed locomotive that was Deccie Fadden's mouth.

"Y'know, the fella who got you suspended off the force there just before Christmas. You said how he goaded you into a bet and whoever wins this game gets his car washed by the other one in front of Garda headquarters. Topless! You said you'd made a terrible mistake and, more than anything, you'd love for us to beat the odds and win this game."

As the Deccie express finally pulled into a station, Bunny looked up and down the line of suddenly concerned faces of a team that hadn't come close to winning for months and who had just been informed that their mentor had bet his dignity on an unlikely upturn in their fortunes.

He threw out an unconvincing smile. "Don't worry about it, lads. Just a bit of craic between two old friends."

"No, boss, you said this Grainger fella was a massive—"

Deccie's attempt to spill what few remaining beans

were left was interrupted by Bunny slamming a hand over his mouth. "Right, boys, time's a ticking. Load up."

All of their concerns were temporarily forgotten as seventeen players attempted to grab one of the precious seats in a minibus that was built to hold twelve.

Bunny watched the scramble, checking no actual war crimes were being committed, before he took his hand off Deccie's mouth and spun him around. He bent down to look his assistant manager directly in the eye. "Fecking hell, Deccie. Do you remember the rest of our little chat?"

Deccie crinkled his brow and counted points off on his fingers. "Have to win the game, this peeler fella is a prick, don't tell the lads, topless washing of car … ah, wait a sec. I see your point. I forgot number three, didn't I?"

Bunny stood up and wiped a hand across his brow. "Jesus Christ and Jackie Charlton! Yes, Deccie, you forgot number three."

"Be fair, boss – I remembered all the other points."

Bunny sighed. "Get on the bus."

"Can I drive?"

"The answer to that question is the same as it was the last million times you asked."

"Do you know what your problem is, boss?"

"You!" snapped Bunny. "Now get moving or I'm not letting you be in charge of the magic sponge."

"How's that positivity thing working out for you so far, boss?"

"'Tis a challenge, Declan. A challenge."

CHAPTER TWO

The minibus descended into an ominous silence as Bunny turned the key in the ignition. The vehicle was unaffectionately known as Bertha. Unaffectionately, as Bunny had only given it that name to stop himself referring to it in more colourful terms. He had long since realised that trying to stop himself swearing entirely in front of the team was unrealistic but, despite the impression given, he did try to keep it to a minimum. The hush was because everyone knew Bunny had no sense of humour whatsoever about Bertha's infuriatingly capricious nature. She could run like a dream for weeks on end only to throw a strop when you really, really needed her to be reliable. They were already running late and, today of all days, Bunny wanted St Jude's putting their best foot forward. They might not win, but at least they could go in and out of there with their heads held high.

The mood was tense as Bunny had already attempted unsuccessfully to start Bertha twice and everybody present knew it was either third time's the charm or half the team had to get back out and push while Sunday shoppers gawped on. Bunny closed his eyes, whispered a prayer to the automotive gods, and turned the key. It was a frozen moment of pause and then, with a cough, a splutter, and a backfire that made a passing greyhound jump into his owner's arms, the engine sprung into life.

The lads cheered and Bunny patted the steering wheel. "Good girl, Bertha. Ye did me proud."

Once she'd started, it was best to give her a few minutes of standing about while she warmed up. In the meantime, there was plenty of admin that needed doing. Bunny looked into the rear-view mirror. The minibus did not have enough seats to carry a fifteen man hurling team, two subs, an assistant manager, and manager/driver/closest thing to a responsible adult. Bunny used to rage about how the makers of minibuses were anti-Gaelic games in that there were just enough seats for a soccer team. Someone had since pointed out to him that there were, in fact, several larger minibuses available, but that was like saying to a homeless person that there was plenty of living space on the moon. St Jude's did not have the kind of budget that could stretch to a fancy new minibus. In fact, St Jude's didn't have any kind of budget. Some parents chipped in when they could, and occasionally Bunny was able to twist some arms of local businesses to throw a few quid in the pot, but mostly he was reliant on whatever grants he could wheedle out of the GAA or putting his hand in his own pocket. They had been approached a couple of times by 'local businessmen' who made their money from less conventional means but, desperate though he was, Bunny had turned those overtures down flat. The whole point of St Jude's was to give him a chance to put some young men on the right path in life and he couldn't preach about staying on the straight and narrow to a bunch of lads running around in jerseys paid for from the proceeds of crime. Morality could be a right pain in the knackers sometimes. The only reason they had Bertha was that two of the leaders of the now-defunct local Cub Scouts had run off together to start a new life in Belgium. It had been quite the scandal, both of the spouses behind whose backs they'd been 'dib, dib, dibbing' had been quoted in a story in the paper. There was talk of a movie.

"Right," said Bunny. "Pre-flight checks ... Has everyone who has a seatbelt clicked it in?"

This was met with a chorus of 'yes, Bunny'.

"And has everybody with a teammate sitting on their lap got a good grip on them?"

This garnered more, if slightly less enthusiastic, confirmations. Technically, they were breaking the rules of the road, but Bunny reasoned whatever danger these boys were in while travelling in Bertha was as nothing compared to the dangers they'd face if left wandering the streets looking for something to do.

"And—"

Bunny found himself interrupted by a camera flash from the seat beside him. "What in the shittin' hell?"

"I'm glad you asked," said Deccie. "I've decided that, as well as being the team's co-manager—"

"Assistant—"

"—I'm also the official photographer and I'm going to document this momentous occasion, boss. I've decided photography is my calling." He held up a hand. "Before you start, Granny already had a word. No nudey stuff, just nice wholesome stuff like wars and that."

"Right, well, that's a relief." Bunny pointed at the disposable camera Deccie was holding. "Where did you get that?"

"I've got like ten of them. Me, Granny and Granda were at Coleen Walsh-from-over-the-road's wedding yesterday and they'd just left a load of these disposable cameras out on the tables."

"You weren't supposed to take them."

"Sure, why did they leave them out then?"

"I'm assuming they wanted people to document the day. Rather than hiring a photographer."

Deccie looked outraged. "As a professional, I'm horrified that they're leaving stuff like that in the hands of amateurs. Not everyone has my eye."

"Oh yeah, you've an eye all right. Just don't take any pictures of me while I'm driving."

"I can't promise that, boss. I have to capture definitive moments wherever they may occur."

"Look at me, Declan." Bunny waited until he did so. "That flash goes off in my face while I'm driving, we are going to have the mother of all definitive moments."

"Noted."

"Speaking of safety, why have you not got your seatbelt on?"

Deccie folded his arms. "I read a thing that says they kill more people than they save."

"Well, we are going to be evening up those numbers a bit because if your seatbelt isn't on in three seconds, you're a dead man."

Deccie mumbled something under his breath, but he

complied. Bunny watched carefully to make sure he was completing the process exactly as instructed. The lad had the kind of sharp instinct for loopholes that would make him a brilliant tax accountant, should anyone ever trust him with their money. Only when he heard the definitive click did Bunny turn his attention to the other front seat passenger who was seated over by the window on the far side of Deccie.

Huey Moore had a particularly unfortunate name, given that he suffered from chronic travel sickness. His poor parents had tried everything – tablets, hypnosis, some weird headband thing – but none of it had worked. At this point, the fella looked ill as soon as he looked at a vehicle. For all of that, he was an indomitable little soul who was not going to let his affliction stop him. He was sitting over there right now, his designated up-chucking bowl gripped in both hands, with a facial expression that was equal parts queasy and determined. Interestingly, the rest of the group had long since got past any urge to make jokes and they were now supportive of Huey in his bi-weekly battle with his own body on the way to every away game. It was partly genuine empathy and partly because he took on the thankless task of being the team's goalie. It took a special mind to see a sliotar, a cork core ball covered in leather that could reach speeds of up to ninety miles an hour, and think, 'I need to get in the way of that thing'. The lad had more stoicism than a monastery of Tibetan monks. Bunny had a growing suspicion that Huey Moore was going to go places in life, even if he would need a large bowl and some wet wipes to get there.

"Are you all right, Huey?"

This was met with a resolute nod.

"Good man, yourself. 'Tis not that long a drive. We'll be there before you know it." Bunny raised his voice again. "Right so – if we are all sitting uncomfortably, we shall begin."

Bunny threw Bertha into gear and with another smoke-belching backfire that caused a certain greyhound to do irreparable damage to his owner's new jumper, off they went.

As always, for the first few minutes of the drive, Bunny said nothing. He was using this time to listen to Bertha for any signs of impending problems while simultaneously getting re-acquainted with her erratic handling. She was not unlike many governments, in that as soon as she hit a bump in the road, she had a tendency to veer wildly to the right. Besides, something in Bunny enjoyed being enveloped in the cheerful chatter of the lads behind him. Inevitably, the talk quickly came around to slagging off the soccer teams that they each supported. The lads were all too aware of Bunny's dislike for the game, so out of deference to him, they'd come up with a system of replacing team names with fruits and vegetables. It wasn't exactly the hardest code to crack. *Bananas were never going to win the FA Cup two years in a row* – but Bunny appreciated them at least making the effort. The only downside was that Liam Boyle supported kumquats, and Bunny had been unsuccessfully attempting to piece together which team that was for over a month now. It was really getting on his nerves. He'd never admit it, but he did occasionally turn on *Match of the Day* when nothing else was on.

Beside him, Deccie cleared his throat in the way that

indicated one of his serious points was coming. "Boss, seeing as this is such a big game—"

"'Tis just another game."

"Pull the other one, boss. You can't big a bigger."

"I think you mean you can't kid a kidder."

"What's that mean?"

"You're the one who said it."

"I didn't, I said big a bigger."

"And what's that mean?"

"It means you can't make a point bigger than my point because my point is already bigger than your point."

"That makes no sense, Deccie."

Deccie threw his hands out. "Makes perfect sense. I'm going to need a ruling on this."

Huey, while he avoided talking as he believed undisturbed regulated breathing helped with his issue, was nevertheless happy to be involved in conversation through the medium of nodding.

Deccie turned to him. "Huey, does 'don't big a bigger' make perfect sense to you?"

He nodded emphatically.

Bunny considered arguing the point, but he decided he didn't have the energy. "Fair enough. What big thing were you going to say?"

"I've been thinking about our tactics."

"Oh, here we go."

Deccie looked at Bunny affronted. "Well, that positivity kick didn't last long, did it?"

"Sorry, Deccie, but before we get into your latest brainwave, let me just temper your expectations. It's a firm no if the plan involves any form of weaponry, sharpening of the hurls or studs, digging a trench or drugging an official. Oh, feck – that reminds me – grab the agenda from the glovebox please, lads."

The agenda was a little notepad that Bunny added to throughout the week, full of lists of things he wanted to bring up on the bus enroute to games. Twelve-year-old boys had the attention spans of stoned goldfish, so Bunny had learned to make use of the time when they were literally a captive audience.

Huey popped the glovebox in front of him open and handed Deccie the notepad and pencil.

"Good, boys. Stick down *referee* please, Declan."

"Are we finally going to bribe a referee like I keep saying?"

"No, we're not," said Bunny, mentally adding that, bar anything else, if they had the budget, Bertha would have a spare tyre. "So, I assume your new strategic masterplan doesn't make it past that test?"

"Actually," said Deccie, "it does."

This caused Huey to glance up momentarily from staring into his bowl.

"Really?" said Bunny. "Well, fire away then."

"OK. Now, this might sound a bit mad, but hear me out. Y'know we have fifteen players on the pitch and they have fifteen players on the pitch?"

"Yeah," said Bunny. "I'm with you so far."

"And how we've got our goalie" – a nod towards Huey – "and they've got their goalie."

"Again, spot on."

"That leaves fourteen players a team out on the field."

"Can't fault your maths. Oh, maths, stick that on the agenda."

"Are you paying proper attention to me?" grumbled Deccie.

"I'm giving you as much attention as I can while keeping us alive and resisting the urge to pullover and throttle the BMW driver that's been flashing his lights behind me for the last two minutes like somehow, he's reserved the road and we're taking his slot. So, my advice, Declan, is stop taking the hump and start making your point."

Deccie tutted. "This is why we need regular management team meetings."

"We would if I had that kind of spare time."

"We're all busy people," said Deccie.

"Really? I'm a member of an underfunded police service who works way more than his allotted hours because otherwise we'd never get any criminals off the streets while simultaneously running this team. You're a young lad who, I know for a fact, doesn't do half his homework because most of the teachers have lost the will to hack their way through your latest jungle of excuses."

"Do you have any idea how long it takes me to come up with those excuses, boss? It'd be easier to just do the homework."

"So why don't you, then?"

"Well, now you're just being ridiculous."

Bunny shook his head. "So, fourteen outfield players per team ..."

"Right, yeah. So, here's my idea. When they have the ball, which, let's be honest, is most of the time" – hard to argue the point on that – "why don't we assign each of our players to follow one of their specific players around for the whole game. Like, you stay with this guy, you stay with that fella, and so on..."

Bunny waited for a few moments, but Deccie said nothing else. "And?"

"And what, boss?"

"What? What you've just described is marking, Deccie."

"You can call it that if you like."

"I call it that. Everyone calls it that. To borrow a phrase from yourself, it's one of the fundamentals of the game. Of all team sports, in fact."

"So why aren't we doing it, then?"

"We..." Bunny took a breath to try to calm himself down. "We are. I mean, we're supposed to be. Are you telling me that you've been the assistant manager for all this time and you've not noticed that?"

"I've not seen any evidence of it."

Bunny couldn't help but clock Huey out of the corner of his eye, nodding in agreement.

"That's as may be, but I'm always telling the lads to do it. What do you think I'm shouting at them throughout the games?"

"To be honest, boss, respectfully, most of us can't figure out what the hell you're saying half the time. With that Cork accent, when you get all wound up, it sounds like someone trying to pull a length of hosepipe out of a lawnmower."

"Are you taking the piss, Deccie?"

"I'm not, boss. It's mainly waving and swearing. D'ye not remember that time at training you got attacked by the bees and it took us all five minutes to figure out what was happening?"

"I..." Bunny found himself speechless, a sense of futility washing over him. Just then, the BMW behind them honked.

"Right, lads," he snarled, "everybody cover your ears and sing *The Wheels on the Bus* now."

"But ..."

"NOW!"

They did as instructed, allowing Bunny to roll down the window and give the honking sod a large piece of his mind, accompanied by a backing track of an unenthusiastic rendition of one of the most pointlessly annoying songs in history. The exchange ended with the other driver flicking Bunny the V's, followed by his face dropping when Bunny flashed his An Garda Síochána ID card in response. He then took great delight in watching the turd's facial expression while Bunny made a great show of taking his numberplate down.

"All right," said Bunny, once Bertha had moved off. "You can stop now, lads."

"Do you feel better after that, boss?" asked Deccie.

"D'ye know what, Deccie? I really do." He guided Bertha up a ramp and onto the M50 motorway. Once they'd successfully merged, Bunny nodded. "Right, Declan. Agenda please."

"What order do you want them in?"

"Surprise me."

"Fair enough. Referee."

"Right, important one this. Lads, pay attention."

The ongoing babble of conversation only abated slightly.

"I said – PAY. ATTENTION." The bus descended into absolute silence. It was so quiet you could hear the various bits of Bertha rattling. "Right. Good. That's the stuff. Now – today St Jude's shall break new ground."

"We're going to actually win?" suggested Wayne O'Brien, accompanied by sniggering.

"Wayne, hilarious as always. I thought you'd be too busy cleaning that day-glow crap off your boots to be sharing your dazzling wit with us."

"You didn't actually say I had to."

"I also didn't tell you not to jump out of the vehicle while it's moving. Some things are just common sense, fella."

"How am I supposed to—"

"You've got a mouth, don't you?"

"You want me to lick it off?" said Wayne, sounding duly outraged as his compatriots laughed and gurned.

"Well, personally, I'd spit on my hand and rub, but I wouldn't like to stifle your creativity. Now, what was I talking about?"

"Referee," prompted Deccie.

"Thank you, Declan. That's right, for the first time today we shall be having a female referee."

He deliberately left a gap and was gratified that nobody filled it. The lads, even someone as unaware as Wayne O'Brien, had been around Bunny long enough to know that he was very hot on certain topics – respect for women being one of the biggest.

"Now," he continued, "I have always said how we must be courteous to all referees—"

Deccie made a scoffing noise. "You said last week's referee was as useless as an umbrella made of bog roll."

"Yes, Declan," said Bunny, through gritted teeth, "but

I said it in private, or at least I said it to you, which is, admittedly, a lot like whispering into a megaphone."

"The week before," said Wayne O'Brien, "you shouted out that the referee was half blind."

"In my defence, he was wearing an eye patch, so that was factually correct, although I will admit it wasn't my finest hour, but the point is ... all of us will treat this lady with absolute respect."

"Is that not sexist?" asked Wayne O'Brien.

"Should you not be busy licking your boots, Wayne?"

Amazingly, without looking around, Bunny was able to hear Wayne open his mouth to retort and being silenced by the sound of the fifteen heads in the back of the minibus simultaneously shaking to discourage him from doing so.

"Good," said Bunny, "now that is settled, what's next on the agenda, Deccie?"

"Maths."

"Ah, yes. Colm Doyle – please make your way to the front of the vehicle."

This was greeted by a cheer from the rest of the team that was twenty percent at Colm Doyle's expense and eighty percent 'thank God this isn't me'.

Colm Doyle was a tall, thin lad who, despite being only twelve years old, had a look about him like he was going bald. He appeared to have been born at forty and was growing into it rapidly. Somebody moved and Colm took the seat directly behind where Deccie was sitting.

"Now, Colm," said Bunny, "a little bird tells me you're failing maths."

"What?" said Colm.

Bunny sighed. "Not an actual bird. It's an expression."

"Would that be Mrs Geraghty who we have for maths?" asked Deccie.

"We'll make a detective of you yet, Declan."

"No offence, boss, but you shouldn't be calling women birds."

"I wasn't … It doesn't … Ah, never mind."

"Come to that," continued Deccie, "she's not exactly what you'd call little."

"If you don't mind," snapped Bunny, "I'm trying to have a conversation with Colm. So, Mr Doyle, have I been misinformed?"

"Maths is rubbish, Bunny," said Colm, with real feeling.

"That may be the case, but it's very important. How are you going to get a job if you can't add up the numbers?"

"S'alright, I'm going to be a plumber just like my da."

"Plumbers need to be able to add up. How are you going to be able to tell how much pipe you need?"

"That's different. That's measuring. I am dead good at measuring."

Deccie spun around in his seat and held up the index fingers of each hand. "How much is that?"

Colm sucked his teeth, proving that being a tradesman really is hereditary. "I make it about eight inches, give or take."

Deccie looked between his two fingers and then nodded. "Fair play, boss. He's good."

"I'm sure he is," said Bunny, "but you use maths for lots of stuff. How are you going to add up how much people owe you?"

"Dad says you just look at how nice the house is, pick

a number, double it and if they don't start screaming, you're golden."

"Well, that's …" Bunny hesitated. Colm Doyle Senior had fixed his boiler last winter for free, so he didn't want to say anything too judgemental. Luckily, a thought struck him. "What about tax?"

"What is tax?"

"Ask your dad about it."

"As it happens, I did exactly that last week."

"And what did he say?"

"He laughed and said, 'what is tax?'"

"Right," said Bunny, finding himself staring at a conversational dead end. "Still, you need to do better in maths. What did you get in the last test?"

"Twelve percent."

"In which case, I want you to do at least forty percent better in the next test."

"How much is that?"

"I'd imagine figuring that out for yourself would be a great first step towards the new improved you."

"Boss," interjected Deccie, "how long until we get there?"

"We'll get there when…" started Bunny, before stopping himself when he glanced down and noticed the look of concern on Deccie's face. He peered over at Huey, who was now doing the kind of breathing you normally associated with going into labour. "We'll be there very soon. Not long at all now. Not long at all."

The intensity of Huey's breathing lessened slightly, but Bunny reckoned they'd only had about twelve minutes at the very most. Luckily, they were only a few minutes away now. "Right, Deccie, what else is on the agenda?"

"It just says 'inspirational speech'."

"Ara shite." Bunny had been meaning to give it more thought, but work had got in the way. He and Butch had been working every hour God sent trying to track down Ian Hendrix. He was a little scrote who had managed to get hold of a list of vulnerable elderly people from the home care company his girlfriend worked for, and he'd been going around robbing their houses, happy to knock about his victims in the process. Even amongst other criminals, there were those who were considered scum. Bunny had gone to bed every night this week dreaming of dangling the little bastard off the side of O'Connell Bridge by his ever-present ratty ponytail. Despite their best efforts, they'd been unable to locate the arsehole and rumour had it he was getting out of the country for good. While he'd wish it to be otherwise, it wasn't Hendrix's fear of the long arm of the law that had prompted his desire to see the world. Sometimes you couldn't help but wonder if there was a higher power moving in mysterious ways. Of all the grannies in all the world, Ian Hendrix had ripped off the one belonging to one Antonio 'Batshit' Cronin. Antonio had just completed a three-year stint in Mountjoy, and he apparently wasn't too worried about going back. Bunny had personally heard Cronin's description of what he would do to Ian Hendrix when he got hold of him and, while it was probably deserved, if brutal, karma, the bit with the particularly creative use of boiled eggs had put Bunny entirely off his lunch. Still, he couldn't think about any of that now. He needed to pull an inspirational speech out of somewhere, and fast.

Inspirational … Inspirational …

He'd been meaning to rent a copy of that *Any Given Sunday* Al Pacino film from a couple of years ago so he could remind himself of that cracking speech Pacino made at the end. It'd been a lot about inches and now that he thought about it, a fair bit about being a middle-aged man. The second part would not resonate with this crowd and the first he could inevitably see getting bogged down in Colm Doyle measuring stuff.

They passed a sign directing them to the ground. Time was running out. Bunny knew more Shakespeare than most people would suspect, but he thought 'once more unto the breach' wouldn't work on a crowd who didn't know what a breach was. Then Deccie would inevitably ask where exactly King Henry was king of and that'd be a whole thing. Along those lines, *Braveheart* might be more relatable, but odds on it would fire the lads up in the wrong way entirely.

When all else fails, there were a couple of things that remained constant about pre-teen boys. "Right, lads, y'know how we always go for chips after a win?"

"That explains why I've been losing weight," said Deccie.

Bunny shifted down a gear and used the opportunity to give Deccie a warning nudge on the leg that now was not the time for him to interrupt.

"This evening, forget chips. When you win – and I've every confidence you will – I'm afraid we won't be going for chips—"

Bunny left a gap for the inevitable groan that duly followed.

"—because … we'll be going for pizza!"

This was met with an ooohh. Shop bought pizza was exotic.

"And not just any pizza, we'll be going to that fancy place that has adverts on the telly."

"Deep crust?" asked Deccie excitedly. "I don't even know what it is, but it sounds like something I'd like."

"Sure! And ..." the sense of excitement in the minibus was even getting to Bunny now, "in celebration of this momentous victory, everyone gets ice cream afterwards too!"

The minibus erupted.

It is rare to hear a loud roar of excitement morph into a groan of disgust, but then, it's not every day that someone throws up into a bowl halfway through it.

"Oh shite," said Bunny. "Sorry, Huey."

CHAPTER THREE

Deccie stood behind Bunny, preparing to latch onto the back of his coat to hold him back if he attempted to charge onto the field. He was on a final warning from the league for what had been termed 'excessive exuberance'. It was his fourth such final warning, but one of these days, final might actually mean final. Deccie was also slightly concerned that Bunny could be heading for one of those heart attacks. He'd watched a programme on telly about them. They looked bad, like heartburn, only worse. According to a bit of paperwork Deccie had accidentally seen once while he was definitely not snooping, Bunny was born in 1969 or something like that, which, given that it was now the year 2001, meant he was really old. He was older than mobile phones, colour TVs and women's rights. Deccie was pretty sure they'd only invented science about 20 years ago. True, his granny and granda were technically older, but they didn't get angry, not like this anyway. Granny got angry like an iceberg, slowly freezing you to death. Bunny went off like a volcano, firing stuff everywhere and causing local villagers to run for the hills or away from the hills, or maybe towards a different hill that wasn't the one that had fire shooting out the top of it. Deccie didn't know much about hills and mountains, only that occasionally one of them was a volcano and that those were deadly in all meanings of the word.

If Bunny had one of these heart attacks, then Deccie was going to have to wallop him on the chest, which he was all right with, and give him the kiss of life, which he was considerably less keen on. He'd do it. Bunny was his friend, after all, but he really didn't want to. He was still figuring out the whole kissing thing and how he felt about it, but he didn't want his first one to involve a big sweaty fella from Cork. He knew that sort of thing did it for other people, and good luck to them, but he was pretty sure it wasn't his bag. Besides, the slagging from the lads would be unbelievable. So, all-in-all, he was dead against Bunny having a heart attack. Unfortunately, the team wasn't doing much to prevent it.

"Tackle him, Barney. Tackle him! Don't get out of his way. This is no time for manners. Go on, Stevie! What was that? For feck's sake, that wouldn't have stopped a plastic bag! C'mon, Dermot, impose yourself. Tackle – No, Dermot, no – the fella with the ball. *With* the ball! We talked about this ... Stop him shooting. Stop him!"

The assembled crowd of parents, bored siblings, people who had absolutely nothing else to be doing on a Sunday morning, and frustrated dogs who couldn't understand why they weren't allowed to join in, collectively 'oohed' in sympathy as the ball skipped past the St Jude's goalie's hurl but got stopped by his ribs.

"Ouch! Good man, Huey. Clear it, lads. Don't let him ..."

Another oohhh. This time, Huey stopped the shot with his head, which was thankfully helmeted. The face mask bore the brunt of the force, but it still snapped back in an unpleasant manner.

"Brilliant, Huey. Clear it, lads. Clear it!"

A third oooohhhhh. This one had a distinct undertone of pained masculinity as Huey saved this shot in a manner that could directly impact there being any Huey juniors in the future.

"For feck's sake, boys. Are you even trying to help him?"

Donnacha Aherne decided to do so by dropping his hurl and offering to pick Huey up, inadvertently getting in his way as he valiantly attempted to throw himself across the goal to save yet another shot.

There was a cheer as, not for the first time, Saint Mungo's scored a goal.

"Jaysus, Donnacha, when I said help him, I meant get rid of the ball!"

"Boss," said Deccie.

"Still, though," said Bunny, remembering his pledge to be more positive, "Well done for picking him up. Good ... erm, teamwork, I suppose. Are you all right, Huey?"

Huey shot them an inexplicably cheery thumbs up.

"That kid has balls of steel."

"Iron, actually," said Deccie.

Bunny looked back at his assistant manager for the first time in a while. "What are you on about?"

"I got him a cup made of iron."

"Actual iron?" asked Bunny.

"Of course," said Deccie, offended at being doubted.

"I mean, that's probably not allowed but, fair play, that's a good idea."

"Thank you."

"I wondered what that clanging noise was. Is it not very uncomfortable?"

"Compared to a high-speed sliotar in the knackers?"

"Point taken. What's the score now?"

"Well," said Deccie, "The good news is, we're only one point behind. The bad news is, we are also five goals behind and seeing as a goal is worth three points that makes us sixteen points behind."

"Thank you, Declan," said Bunny gruffly. "I do understand how the scoring system works."

"Right, only you shouted out after their last score that the next goal was important, and, by my reckoning, it isn't."

"I was trying to be inspirational."

"Oh, right. Good one, boss."

Bunny glanced down at Deccie again.

"I'm trying to be positive, too."

"It doesn't suit you."

"Yeah, I felt that as soon as I said it."

Bunny shrugged. "Thanks for trying."

"Look on the bright side, boss …"

There was a pause as they watched the St Jude's players trudge back into position for the puck-out to restart the game. They looked deflated.

Eventually Bunny said, "Deccie, y'know when you say, 'look on the bright side'?"

"Yes, boss."

"You're generally supposed to follow up by saying what the bright side actually is."

"Really?"

"Yes."

"Shite. I wish I'd known that before I said it. I'm not a miracle worker."

DI Grainger waved cheerily across to Bunny from the other sideline. "I really thought you'd give us more of a game than this."

"'Tis not over yet."

Grainger laughed. "Says who?"

"You're a shining example of sportsmanship, Detective Inspector."

"Can't take a little joke, Detective. Where's that famous McGarry sense of humour?"

"If I want a laugh, I just look up your arrest record."

Deccie pulled at Bunny's coat. "Sorry to interrupt your friendly banter with the gobshite, boss, but …" Bunny followed Deccie's pointed finger. Johnny Murphy was bent over, both hands on his knees. "Ah crap, Johnny's asthma is playing up." Bunny waved his hand. "Referee."

She glanced over in his direction.

"Substitution please, come on in, Johnny."

He turned to what remained of their bench. He'd been forced to send Dave Blake on for Paschal Quinn in the first half. They could ill-afford to lose him, Paschal being one of the few players on the team who had shown any understanding of where the opposition's goal might be, but he'd been taken out by a brutally high challenge. Bunny hadn't been able to complain about it much, given that it had come from one of his own teammates. Bunny had dropped several hints to Dermot's dad that he might need to get tested for being colour blind, but nothing had been done so far. Still, at least Dermot was tackling people. Besides, St Jude's had so little of the ball that Dermot catching one of his own teammates in possession was really spectacularly bad luck. Grainger, standing on the sideline had attempted to make some hilarious remark about that, but Bunny had deliberately kept talking loudly so as not to hear it. The prick had sent his team out there going for goals instead of trying to score points – a dick move to try to run up the score against an inferior opponent.

Having used Dave early doors, Bunny was left with their one remaining substitute.

"Right," he said clapping his hands together as he turned around, "'tis time to pull out the big guns!"

Rían Stark looked hurt by the remark. Bunny winced. The lad was a sensitive soul, and Bunny had made it very clear to all and sundry that his weight issues were not to be referenced. It didn't help that he was sitting behind them on a deckchair, working his way through a large bag of Tayto crisps. There was something almost magical about Rían. You could be shipwrecked on a desert island and somehow, three weeks in, you'd walk around a palm tree to find him polishing off an ice lolly.

"Sorry, Rían, I didn't mean … I meant you're our secret weapon!"

"I am?" asked Rían.

"He is?" asked Deccie.

"He is," said Bunny, shooting Deccie a warning look. "I'm going to stick you on for Johnny."

"But," said Rían, "Johnny plays on the wing. And he's

marking that guy who keeps knocking the ball in for the fella who keeps scoring all the goals."

"Precisely. We stop him. We stop them. And you're the man for the job."

"Really?" Rían's forehead scrunched up in consternation. "But he's way faster than me."

"Exactly. He's faster than Johnny, too. That's why his asthma is playing up. We've been approaching this all wrong. There's no point chasing after someone who's faster than you. Do you know what the definition of insanity is?"

"That fella on Capel Street who throws his own poo at buses?" asked Deccie.

"No," snapped Bunny through gritted teeth. "It's doing the same thing over and over again and expecting a different result. Einstein said that." Bunny jabbed a finger in the direction of the field. "Maybe he's faster than you. Taller than you. Fitter than you. But you've got something he'll never have …"

"Type two diabetes?" interjected Deccie.

"Heart," said Bunny. "You've got more heart than any two of them Southside soft lads with their correctly fitting jerseys and thirty quid haircuts. Now go out there and show them what you got."

Rían nodded furiously, his face a mask of grim determination. It slipped a little as it took him three attempts to get out of his deckchair, but he appeared to regather himself once he'd found his feet. Bunny and Deccie watched in silence as he ran across the field to take up his position, high-fiving Johnny with more vigour than was necessary as he passed him trudging off the field. It was Deccie who spoke first. "Thirty quid haircuts?"

"I dunno. I had to come up with something."

"Fair enough. Did Einstein really say that, though?"

"Course he did. Famous for it."

"Interesting."

"I'll tell you something about Einstein though, Deccie, that a lot of people don't know."

"What's that?"

"He never had to coach an under-12s hurling team." Bunny clapped his hands together loudly. "Right, c'mon now, lads. All still to play for. The score is nil-nil."

"Nah, boss," shouted back Colm Doyle. "They're miles ahead of us. I've been counting. I make it they're a point and five goals up on us. That's ..."

He dropped his hurling stick and looked at his fingers, a look of concentration on his face.

"It was a figure of speech, Colm!" shouted Bunny, before he got to the idea of taking his boots and socks off. "Don't worry about it." A thought struck Bunny. "You see that blonde fella in midfield?"

Colm nodded.

"He's a leak, and I want you to plumb him. Plumb the living shite out of him."

To Deccie's surprise, the young man's eyes lit up, and he nodded intently. "Right, boss." He ran off to find his man.

"Pick up your hurl, Colm," shouted Bunny. "Your hurl."

Colm came back and got it, the fire still burning in his eyes.

"Nicely done, boss," said Deccie. "If you're looking for similar stuff, Donnacha wants to be a butcher, like his uncle, when he grows up. You could get him to chop the legs off that little nippy fella who keeps scoring all the goals."

"Tempting, but no."

They watched as Huey took the puck-out, catching it better than he had all day. The ball hurtled high and long, heading for the left wing. The boy marked by Rían Stark rose and caught the sliotar one-handed. He then looked up to see the considerable bulk of Rían hurtling towards him like a demented boulder of bad intentions rolling downhill. His opponent yelped as he blindly attempted a pass behind him to nobody in particular before diving out of the way.

The ball spilled loose, and the St Mungo's midfielder moved in smoothly, intent on flicking it deftly up onto his hurl, but he never got the chance. Colm Doyle slammed into him with a shoulder charge that left him poleaxed on the ground in front of the opposition bench.

"Referee!" screeched Grainger from the far sideline in protest. The ref tapped her shoulder. "Shoulder to shoulder. Perfectly legal."

Colm, meanwhile, was not waiting around to admire his handiwork. With a determination that had been entirely absent from his play up until this point, he walloped the ball with everything he had, sending it skittering down the field.

Jason Phillips pushed his glasses up his nose, watching the ball coming his way with a look of concentration on his face.

"Oh shite," exclaimed Bunny. Two of the opposition were heading towards Jason from either side, intent on making him the meat in a very unhappy sandwich. Bunny tried to shout something but 'look out you're about to get crushed' was too many words to get out in the time allowed. He only got as far as "Whatchathething—"

The ball reached Jason just before his would-be tacklers. He let it roll onto his hurl and then fell forward, shot-putting the ball high over his shoulders as he did so. As he fell, the two slices of bread slammed into each other in a messy, high-carb, collision.

Bunny watched, mouth gawping, as the ball arched through the air towards the St Mungo's goal. Deccie grabbed onto the sleeve of his coat. "Fucking hell, boss!"

Wayne O'Brien stood in front of the St Mungo's goal, entirely oblivious to the goings on down the pitch. He'd got hold of an orange highlighter from somewhere and he was trying to go for a tricky two-tone design on his boots. The St Mungo's defence, untroubled as they were, had got sucked into watching him work and giving advice. Wayne looked up at the sound of his name being roared to see Bunny and Deccie pointing at the sky.

"What?" he shouted back.

"The ball," screamed Bunny, "the fecking ball!"

Wayne looked up and sighted the ball passing over his head now on its descent. Then his instincts took over. Unfortunately, he did not have the instincts of a hurler, which was why he dropped his hurl, along with the orange highlighter, and he dashed forward towards the St Mungo's goal. The goalie was coming out to meet him, intent on closing down the angle. With a diving lunge, Wayne propelled himself forward, the sliotar meeting the front of his helmet and flying upwards again, arching over the despairing fingertips of the St Mungo's goalie before the two of them collided and tumbled to the ground.

They both watched helplessly as the sliotar dropped, bounced and then, as if in slow motion, trickled towards the St Mungo's goal. The world seemed to stand still as with its very last ounce of momentum it rolled over the line.

The entire St Jude's team erupted into cheering and Bunny realised he was hugging Deccie while they jumped up and down. It wasn't like they hadn't scored a goal before. Back in the golden era when Paul Mulchrone had played for them, they'd been knocking them in for fun. But that felt like a long time ago now.

"Wonderful stuff, lads," hollered Bunny. "Wonderful stuff. That's the spirit! The fightback starts now!"

"Bullshit," screamed Grainger from the far sideline as he stomped onto the field towards the referee. "That's bullshit. You can't score a header in hurling."

"There's no law against it," said the referee.

"Course there is."

"No, there isn't," chimed in Bunny.

Grainger glared across at Bunny. "Shut up, ye fat prick."

"Right," said the referee, "we'll have none of that. Get back to your sideline now or I'll book you for dissent."

"You can't do that."

"Yes, I can. I'm the referee."

"Ah, you're not a proper referee."

"Really?" she said, before shooting her hand into her pocket and producing a yellow card. "Well, this is still a proper card. You're booked!"

Grainger held his hands up. "Whoa, whoa, whoa! Calm down there, love. Can't we have a civilised discussion about the rules?"

"Don't 'love' me," she snapped back. "It's ref or referee."

"Jesus," said Grainger. "Someone's in a mood. That time of the month, is it?"

A weird moment of silence descended upon the field. When the referee spoke again, it was barely above a whisper and yet it carried like a sonic boom across the field. "Excuse me?"

Bunny grabbed Deccie's shoulder. "Pay attention, Deccie. You're about to learn a valuable life lesson."

CHAPTER FOUR

About forty minutes later, Bunny clambered into the front seat of Bertha and slammed the door shut. "Right, lads, who's up for some pizza?"

This was met with a roar of approval from all around him.

"And ice cream?" asked Deccie.

"And ice cream," confirmed Bunny. "I'm a man of my word."

This was met with another roar.

Bunny glanced across at Huey, who was sitting at the other end of the front seat, gripping his bowl as always. "Oh, sorry, Huey, I didn't mean to, y'know …"

"Oh, no," said Huey. "No worries. I just … I mean, can I ask … We didn't actually win the game though, did we?"

Bunny nodded. "That's an excellent question. In fact, pay attention, lads. There are a couple of big life lessons to take away from today" – Bunny held a finger up – "Number one – victory comes in many forms. Sometimes, it's winning a hard-fought battle and doing so with a bit of class. Sometimes it's losing with good grace, especially if the other side are being gobshites about it. And sometimes, and admittedly, this is a bit of a rarer one, but sometimes, victory is having your game abandoned after the referee gives the arsehole in charge of the other team an almighty boot in the bollocks."

This was greeted by another massive cheer. Bunny couldn't help grinning from ear to ear. The memory of seeing Grainger rolling around on the ground was going to warm the cockles of his heart on many a cold night. And it wouldn't just do so for him, young Deccie Fadden having proven that he might just have the instincts to be a war photographer after all, having captured it for posterity. He'd used up an entire disposable camera on it. The shot of Grainger begging for mercy when the referee was being held back by the quickest thinking of the St Mungo's parents would be particularly delightful. It occurred to Bunny that he could pay the no doubt sizeable bill for feeding the entire team fancy pizza if he got a load of copies of those pictures made and sold them around the force. Grainger was not a popular man.

"Which brings me, lads, to important life lesson number two." He held up a second finger. "Now, I assume somebody in school has explained to you what is meant by a lady's 'time of the month'?"

This was met with enough nods that Bunny could choose to interpret it as universal. If not, they'd explain it to one another later on and more or less get the general idea across.

"Right. Good. The big lesson to take away from today is you never ever, ever, ever, bring it up in conversation. I mean ever. This piece of advice should be one of them public service announcement things on the TV, like not trying to get your frisbee out of a power line or the dangers of drowning in a slurry pit. Just, trust me on this; never ever mention it, OK?"

This was met with solemn nods all round.

"Good."

"I have a question," said Deccie.

Bunny sighed. He knew it had been too good to be true. "Go on then."

"What in the hell is a slurry pit?"

"Oh," said Bunny. He hadn't known exactly what he'd expected, but this definitely wasn't it. "It's a thing they have on farms. 'Tis a big container mainly full of animal shite."

"And people drown in that?"

"Yeah, I'm afraid so. There's a case every few years."

Deccie shook his head. "I've said it before, and I'll say it again. People from the country are mental. I mean, why would you go swimming in that in the first place?"

"They don't—" started Bunny before being interrupted by Wayne O'Brien pointing excitedly out the window.

"Boss, boss, boss!"

They all saw where he was pointing. DI Grainger, an ice bag applied to his nether regions, was walking gingerly back to his car.

He looked up at the sound of a detective of his acquaintance pretending to be a bugler, giving a soulful rendition of the 'Last Post' while a minibus full of grinning pre-teens saluted him.

"Oh, piss off!"

CHAPTER FIVE

Bunny wiped a tear from his eye. "All right, c'mon. Stop it now, stop it!"

As he'd suspected, Deccie had clearly spent the majority of the time since their last minibus journey working on his repertoire of fart impressions, and it had not been time spent in vain. Not only that, he'd clearly been paying considerably more attention to current affairs to work on his material, as there were some shrewd political points amidst the gastric fireworks. Bunny guessed most of his audiences didn't get a lot of the references, but the genius of the medium was that even without understanding the nuance, twelve-year-old-boys loved fart noises more than life itself.

"Hang on, boss," said Deccie. "I've got one more."

"Seriously, we're on O'Connell Street now. The pizza place is just up on the corner here. I need to figure out where to park."

"One more. It's a good one."

Bunny shook his head but couldn't help grinning. "All right, one more."

"Grand. This one is a question for you, lads. Who am I?" *Fart* "Oh jaysus, me nuts," *fart* "Oh God, them St Jude's boys ruined me," *fart*. "Never mention periods." *Fart, fart, fart*. "Oh, that Bunny McGarry is a pain in my arse almost as bad as the one in my bollocks."

Someone behind them honked as Bunny stopped the minibus, unable to trust himself to drive straight. It wasn't the most sophisticated humour in the world, but you could say this for Deccie, he certainly knew his audience. People were falling out of their seats in fits of hysterics. Huey was doubled over with laughter, clutching his bowl hard to his chest.

Someone honked behind them again.

Bunny lowered the window and stuck out a hand to wave them by.

Outside, a light rain had started to fall, adding an additional twist of discomfort to an already bitterly cold Sunday in January. It was nearly lunchtime and town was fairly busy, Sunday shopping now in full flow after the first payday of the new year.

He still had no idea where they were going to park, but ...

Bunny stopped dead. A laugh caught in his throat.

They'd seen each other at exactly the same time. Their eyes locked. What were the odds? Standing there on the far side of O'Connell Street, as real as life itself and twice as ugly, Ian 'Bastard' Hendrix. The granny-robbing scumbag, poised to step into the open driver-side door of a green Peugeot 306, wore an expression of utter shock. There was a roof rack on the top of the car with cases strapped to it. Someone was planning a long trip. In the passenger seat sat Ciara, Ian's girlfriend, who had tearfully sworn on everything under the sun that they were no longer an item. Butch had called that one right enough. Unfortunately, woman's intuition had not been enough to hold her on.

The two men stared at each other; the world frozen around them. "Quiet, lads," hissed Bunny, his hand resting on the door handle. The hubbub only subsided a little. He watched Ian glancing around. They were both doing the same calculations. Could Bunny reach him before Ian was in the car and away?

"Quiet," repeated Bunny. This time, Deccie caught the tone in Bunny's voice and shushed the lads into silence.

He could see Ian and Ciara were having a conversation while Ian kept his eyes firmly on Bunny. He noticed her looking in his direction and then throwing her hands up in the air in exasperation, her *nice young girl led astray* defence having now gone up in flames. Odds on, she was the brains of the outfit, brains having never been something Ian Hendrix had been known for.

Bunny spoke in a low, calm voice. "Everybody double-check your seatbelts and hold on extra tight to anyone who hasn't got one."

"Why ..." started Wayne O'Brien, the rest of his question lost under a collective gasp of shock as Bertha lurched forward. Ian had dived into the driver's seat of the Peugeot. With a squeal of tyres, it took off up O'Connell Street, attracting the attention of passers-by.

"Hold on," roared Bunny as he cut across two lanes of

traffic, laying on the horn as he did so. Pedestrians dived out of the way as Bertha mounted the kerb onto the central paved area that divided the two lanes of traffic heading north from the two heading south, causing everyone in the minibus to bounce up in the air. There was an unpleasant scrapping noise as Bertha's undercarriage ground against the stone. With a shuddering thwack, the back wheel mounted the kerb too.

"Sorry," screamed Bunny out the window to the world in general.

"What the hell, boss?" roared Deccie.

"That Peugeot has a very bad man in it."

"And this minibus has a hurling team in it. You're not going to catch him."

The minibus juddered sickeningly as it thumped down onto the south-running side of the street, while the front bumper hit the ground with a screeching protest of metal and a shower of sparks.

"I don't need to catch him," shouted Bunny. "I just need to stay close and Sunday traffic will do the rest. Grab my phone from my coat."

Despite what you see in the movies, running a red light is an activity that rarely goes well. The Peugeot had used its head start to attempt to do just that. Hendrix had struck a Nissan that had been foolish enough to assume a green light meant *go*, and the Peugeot now had to reverse before attempting to weave around the vehicle, its apoplectic driver standing by her car, hands held out in disbelief. Bunny, his own fist still firmly wedged on the horn, wove around the traffic as best he could. They were still too far back. "C'mon, c'mon – he's getting away."

"Who am I ringing?" asked Deccie.

"999 of course."

"Right and—"

"Hang on," screamed Bunny, as, absent any other ideas, he had remounted the central reservation to try to catch up with Hendrix. Every passenger screamed as Bertha's right wheel clanked onto the high kerb. Bunny caught a flash of a hub cap making a break for freedom in his side-view mirror.

"Keep driving like this," hollered Deccie, "and I'd imagine the pigs will be here soon."

"Garda, not pigs," said Bunny through gritted teeth as he jerked the bus left to avoid hitting the pole of a streetlight, leaving them half-on, half-off the paved area, trundling awkwardly alongside the line of traffic, clipping the odd wing mirror as they went. Bunny revved the engine to get the minibus's right wheel over a metal bar that protruded from a bike rack.

The entire minibus yelled in alarm as Bertha begin to tip to the left.

"Shite," roared Bunny, "everybody lean to the right!"

He'd had no idea if that would work, but thankfully, Bertha managed to steady herself. A bloke on a bicycle dived out of their way and Bunny caught sight of the Peugeot up ahead. It had hit a wall of traffic at the lights up on O'Connell Bridge.

"Gardaí please," hollered Deccie into the phone, "and we're probably going to need an ambulance or two as well."

"We've got the prick!" screamed Bunny, now only one block away from their target. They bounced back onto the street again, minus the driver's side wing mirror that had come off much the worse in a collision with the base of a traffic light. On the far side of the bus, there was a scrape of metal as Bertha ruined somebody's paint job.

"Sorry," shouted Bunny again.

On the far side of the front seat, Bunny heard Huey throwing up into his bowl. "Better out than in, Huey," said Bunny, not taking his eyes off the prize in front of him. "Better out than in."

Ian Hendrix had now realised he was trapped behind the wall of traffic, because nobody was getting out of his way, no matter how much he honked. A double-decker bus sat to the right of him, further hemming them in. As Bunny headed towards it, the Peugeot was thrown suddenly into reverse. If they could get down Abbey Street, they'd be gone and nothing Bunny could do would stop him.

"O'Connell Street," screamed Deccie into the phone, "there's at least one madman on the loose."

"Oh shite," roared Bunny. "Hang on, lads."

With a crunch of metal, Bertha rammed into the back of the Peugeot. It was like Bunny had told Rían Stark. Speed would only get you so far if your opponent was willing to throw a whole lot of bulk at you. Bertha might not be able to outrun anyone, but the old girl had bulk and a whole lot of momentum. They all lurched forward, and there was a great deal of swearing as Bertha rear-ended the Peugeot into the back of a large van in front of it, wedging it firmly in place.

Bunny turned around in his seat. "Is everybody all right?"

"Are we still getting pizza?" asked Wayne O'Brien from somewhere in the mass of bodies.

Bunny took that as a yes. "Stay here."

He was unbuckled and out of the minibus in time to see Ian Hendrix pulling one of the suitcases down from the roof rack and then making a run for it.

Before he got six feet away, Bunny shoulder charged him into the side of the bus, sending the case flying out of Ian's hand. It walloped against the side of the bus with a jangle. Bunny guessed it contained the valuables from Ian's despicable crime spree that he'd not yet sold. As he landed, Bunny got a brief flash of wide-eyed faces pressed up against the window of the double-decker as they tumbled to the ground. Ian found his feet quickly and his flailing kick caught Bunny square in the stomach, knocking the wind out of him.

He tried to run for it, but Bunny grabbed hold of his left leg and held on for dear life. "Not today, gobshite."

He couldn't see his opponent, but Bunny sensed something in the movement from above that made him instinctively duck away. That was what caused the knife to slice into the shoulder of his jumper instead of his face, where it had been aimed. Bunny reared back and used the side of the bus to regain his feet. Ian Hendrix stood a few feet from him, blood trickling from his forehead, the blade in his right hand and a wild look in his eye. His desire for vengeance having superseded his instinct to run.

"You bastard," he hissed.

"Sorry, Ian. I know you prefer fighting pensioners."

"Come on, Ian!" shouted Ciara, somewhere to Bunny's left. He wasn't sure if she meant that in the 'let's get the hell out of here' or 'get him!' sense of the words, and he certainly didn't have the time to ask.

The thing about fighting someone who has a knife when you don't is that they're thrilled about the knife bit. Like how when you've got a hammer, everything is a nail. When you've got a knife, everything is something you can stick a knife into. That meant as the non-knife-wielder, you just had to worry about the knife, whereas they had to worry about every bit of you. Only, they probably weren't worried enough due to the aforementioned knife-based confidence. This was why when Bunny feinted towards the blade, Ian bought it hook, line and sinker and lunged forward to stab him, getting the sole of Bunny's left boot smashed into the side of his right kneecap for his trouble. As Ian crumpled to the ground with a wail of anguish, Bunny's right fist came around and caught him sweetly on the jaw, sending him sprawling sideways.

All-in-all, it was going surprisingly well. Too well. Bunny caught the flash of movement from the corner of his eye, but by then it was too late. Stupid. He'd been so shocked to see Ian, he'd not clocked the other guy sitting in the back seat. It must have taken him a while to extricate himself from the back of the Peugeot thanks to it being a three-door, but now he had, he'd caught Bunny cold. Something hard and heavy smashed into the back of Bunny's head, and the world lurched nauseatingly out of focus. He stumbled into the side of the double-decker and then dropped to the ground.

His vision came back into focus for a moment, and he looked up to see a big man he'd never seen before standing over him. They had wondered if Ian had an accomplice. He had a shaven-head and was wearing a dark-green bomber jacket. As he raised something over his head, Bunny started to black out.

The last thing he heard before he lost consciousness was a surprised yelp.

CHAPTER SIX

"Bunny," said a soft voice. "Bunny. Wake up. C'mon, wakey wakey ..."

He turned his head, unwilling to leave the soft embrace of sleep just yet.

When the voice spoke again, it was in a lower, less kindly register. "Cork is a shithole."

His eyes flew open to see Detective Pamela 'Butch' Cassidy smiling down at him.

Bunny coughed and then spoke. "Ara, just my luck – I get to heaven and all the angels are lesbians."

"You seriously think you're going to heaven?"

"Well, if you qualify as an angel, anything is possible."

Bunny put a hand to his head and confirmed that there was a large bandage wrapped around it. "Jaysus, who hit me?"

"Would you believe some big sod with a tyre iron?"

"I would, I ..." Bunny tried to sit up as his recollection cleared. "The lads!"

"Relax," said Butch, placing a placatory hand on his

shoulder. "Everyone is OK. Well, at least everyone you like. Ian Hendrix and his amigos aren't that OK at all."

Bunny continued to sit up and Butch took a moment to assist him, moving the pillows to support him. He took in his surroundings for the first time. He was in a private room and judging by the view out the window, he reckoned this was the Mater Hospital. "How long have I been out for?"

"It's Monday afternoon."

"God, really?"

"Ah, you're always saying you don't sleep so well. Think of this as a nice lie-in and you didn't even have to get drunk to achieve it."

"Still got the hangover, though." Bunny smacked his dry lips. "My mouth's like the Sahara."

Butch picked up a glass of water from the bedside cabinet and held it in front of him, straw out. He took a sip.

"Ta."

"Happy to serve"

"I still don't understand what happened," said Bunny.

"How much do you remember?" asked Butch.

"We were on O'Connell Street, after playing the game against St Mungo's ..." His eyes lit up. "Did you hear—"

"About Grainger's testicular encounter with authority? Yes, everyone has heard about that. He wanted to press charges, but I believe the commissioner told him to cop himself on and stop attempting to be an even bigger embarrassment to the force than he already is."

"Glad to hear it," said Bunny. "So, I was on O'Connell Street and then, by pure fluke, who do I see but Ian 'Bastard' Hendrix. We spent the last two weeks doing everything we can to find the little shite with no success, and then he just appears right in front of me as if by magic. I couldn't believe it."

"I'd imagine he couldn't either. It's always the way, though. How many serial killers have been caught because of a broken light on a car or an innocuous coincidence? It'd almost make me believe in God."

"To be fair, if this was God, next time I hope he drops something like this in my lap when I'm not driving a minibus full of kids." Bunny winced. "Christ, I can't believe I actually gave chase."

Butch waved a hand dismissively. "Ah, kids love a bit of excitement. Imagine how much they're going to enjoy telling this story for the rest of their lives. You can't buy something like that."

"And they're ...?"

Butch could see where his mind was heading. "Again. Absolutely fine. Not a scratch on them, which is more than can be said for your minibus, I'm afraid."

"Ah, crap."

"I've some good news on that front. He doesn't want it known, but the commish has told the garage boys to sort it out for you."

"Really?"

"Yeah, I guess he reckons he owes you one after a couple of your recent adventures. So, you managed to chase old Ian boy down?"

"I did," confirmed Bunny, "and then ... Well, I think I took him down, but things get a little hazy from there." He noticed Butch's wide grin. "What?"

"Well, as luck would have it, I can fill in the gaps for you from that point as" – she reached into the pocket of her coat and pulled out a pile of photographs – "the whole encounter was captured for posterity by a promising young photographer."

"You're kidding?"

"Nope. Deccie might have found his calling. These are copies, obviously – the originals are in evidence, and I'd imagine several other copies will be doing the rounds for years to come." She began handing Bunny pictures. "There's you tackling Mr Hendrix into the side of the bus. There's the two of you scrapping on the ground. Oh, by the way, worth keeping an eye on the old one there on the bus in the blue anorak. Everyone else is gawping out the window in every picture and, swear to God, she just keeps looking at her watch, like '*Bergerac* is on the telly in twenty minutes, can we move this along?'"

Bunny looked at the picture. It was weird seeing himself fighting somebody like this. Butch handed him the next picture. "Here's Ian, the naughty little scamp, pulling a knife on you. Here's you booting him in the knee. Excellent action shot that one ... You're about to throw a dig into his jaw in this one. And there's him lying on the ground. Deccie himself was bitterly disappointed at not getting a snap of the punch landing, but you can't have everything ..." Butch handed him another photo. "Here's that prick in the bomber jacket running in to blindside you. Gary Nolan, by the way, from Tallaght. He's already been inside for assault and he's a proper scumbag. No idea how he and Ian even know each other. There must be some website where arseholes can connect with their soulmates." Butch said nothing as she handed him the next picture. It was of himself pitching forward, having been blindsided with a vicious blow from a tyre iron to the back of the head.

"God," said Bunny, "he could have killed me."

"I know," Butch replied. "Luckily, he hit you on your head, which, as we all know, is thicker than concrete. Speaking as your partner, though, this is why you're supposed to stick to law enforcement while on the job. You don't do well without adult supervision."

"Fair point."

"Anyway, here's the prick standing over you with a tyre iron, and you're about to get your name on a plaque on the wall. And here comes the cavalry …"

Nolan, the guy in the bomber jacket spun around in shock when the first hurly hit him, but, as the sequence of photos revealed, he quickly crumbled under the sustained assault of a pack of pre-teen, hurly wielding maniacs literally falling over each other to wallop him. It was notable that when he hit the ground, they did not stop. In fact, Ian Hendrix's attempt to limp away in the confusion meant he got in on the action too.

"Jesus," said Bunny. "They're like wild animals. Believe you me, they've never shown this level of teamwork previously."

"Yeah. My favourite is the next one. This is the shot of shots. Ciara, the conniving little witch, tried to grab the suitcase of loot and run." She handed Bunny another photograph.

"Is that …?"

Butch giggled. "What I am reliably informed is a bowl of warm sick being hurled over her. By all accounts, she did not take it well. There're a few more …"

Butch handed him a quick sequence of photos. In

them, the angle changed as it got closer to the prime figures of Nolan and Hendrix on the ground, both now balled up to protect themselves.

Neither Butch nor Bunny said anything. That way, neither of them had to admit that this was Deccie clearly taking the opportunity to put the literal boot in on both men. The last few shoots were of gardaí in uniform, turning up and dragging wild-eyed hurlers off their opponents.

"The first guards on the scene had a bit of a time of it getting your boys to lower their weapons. They also all wanted to go in the ambulance with you."

Bunny didn't know what to say to that.

"That's the end of it," said Butch, taking the pile of photos back out of his hands.

"Wow. That's … that's quite something."

"Yeah, it's going to make one hell of a flip book."

"The lads aren't going to get into trouble, are they?"

Butch shook her head. "Nah, the dynamic duo got off with way fewer injuries than they deserve. Besides, these pricks put helpless pensioners in the hospital. No defence lawyer in the country is going to be pushing the boat out to get them off. They're going to get the shittiest of shitty deals, and then when they're in prison, well, we all know how nutters feel about their grannies."

"So, all's well that ends well."

"Oh no," said Butch. "You're not getting off that easy. Are you feeling up to visitors?"

"I suppose," said Bunny.

"Good," said Butch, standing up and heading over to the door, "because much to the annoyance of the matron, you've got eighteen of them." She opened the door. "You can—" before she could finish the sentence, the entire St Jude's Under-12s hurling team rushed into the room, led by their assistant manager.

They all spoke at once. "Are you all right, boss? How's the head? Did you brain leak out? We beat the crap out of them fella, did ye see? Huey says he reckons his travel sickness is cured now. Can we beat up some more people?"

Bunny held his hands up. "Lads, lads, lads – a bit of quiet, please. 'Tis great to see you all. I'm grand. Thanks for popping in to see me and for, y'know, helping out yesterday."

"Those were exactly the kind of tactics I've been saying we should use," said Deccie.

"Well, we're not. So don't go getting any ideas. Should you lot not all be in school?"

"It's five o'clock," said Donnacha.

"Oh right. Well, doing homework then?"

"We didn't get any homework," added Colm Doyle. "Not even maths."

"Yeah," said Wayne, "we're heroes now. We've been in the paper and everything."

Bunny looked at Butch. "Really?"

"It's fine," she said. "It got some very sympathetic reporting."

"The lady called us plucky," said Huey.

"Well," replied Bunny, "you've been called worse. And …" He stopped. "What's that smell?"

He noticed the sea of grins looking back at him and then Deccie, as elected spokesman, spoke up. "Well, a promise is a promise, and it turns out they deliver." He raised his voice and turned to the door. "You can come in now."

The door opened and two smiling nurses came in carrying large piles of pizza boxes, cheered on by the team.

Chaos ensued as the boxes were grabbed and then traded and squabbled over. Butch looked down at Bunny. "The lads down the station all chipped in."

"Thank them for me."

"Do you want a slice?"

Bunny shook his head and smiled. "Nah, I'm all right. This is good for me, though."

"Oh," said Butch, raising her voice, "speaking of which … Are you forgetting something, lads?"

Rían Stark froze, a slice of pizza halfway into his mouth. "She's not asking us to pray or wash our hands or some shite like that, is she?"

"No," said Butch, nodding her head towards the door, "the other thing."

"Oh right," said Deccie, dropping his pizza box on Bunny's bed. "Donnacha, go get it."

Donnacha nodded and headed back out the door.

Deccie raised himself up to his full height. "We wanted to get you a present for, y'know, stuff, and Donnacha's auntie works in that big shop in town, and she got us a really good deal."

Donnacha pushed back through the door, now carrying an A1-sized frame.

"It's something to remember us by," said Colm Doyle.

"And if I do say so myself," added Deccie, "my finest piece of work to date."

With a slightly awkward flourish, Donnacha turned

the large frame around and held it above his head to reveal a picture. They all cheered.

Bunny laughed so hard his head hurt.

There before him was a magnificent shot of DI Grainger getting booted in the knackers by a referee who had taken just about enough of his crap.

Eventually, Bunny wiped his eyes and regained the power of speech. "'Tis perfect, lads. Just perfect."

FREE BOOK

Hello again lovely reader-person,

So there you go, I hope you've enjoyed frolicking around Dublin with Bunny, Deccie, Bertha and the gang in this novella. Thanks for buying it and taking the time to read it.
Bunny will be back later in the year.

If you need a Caimh fix before then make sure you've signed up for my monthly newsletter for free short stories, audio, and the latest goings on in the Bunnyverse.

You'll also get a copy of my short fiction collection called *How To Send A Message*, which features several stories featuring characters from my books. To sign up go to my website:

www.WhiteHairedIrishman.com

FREE BOOK

The paperback costs $10.99/£7.99/€8.99 in the shops but you can get the e-book for free just by signing up to my newsletter.

Oooh, and you can also listen to the Bunnycast and The Stranger Times podcasts too for more audio exclusives and short stories. They're available from all the usual places or through my website or **thestrangertimes.co.uk.**

Cheers muchly and thanks for reading,

Caimh

ALSO BY CAIMH MCDONNELL

The Increasingly Inaccurately Titled Dublin Trilogy

A Man With One of Those Faces (Book 1)

The Day That Never Comes (Book 2)

Angels in the Moonlight (Book 3/prequel)

Last Orders (Book 4)

Dead Man's Sins (Book 5)

Firewater Blues (Book 6)

The Family Jewels (Book 7)

Escape from Victory (Book 7.5)

McGarry Stateside (featuring Bunny McGarry)

Disaster Inc (Book 1)

I Have Sinned (Book 2)

The Quiet Man (Book 3)

MCM Investigations (featuring Brigit & Paul)

The Final Game (MCM Investigations 1)

Deccie Must Die (MCM Investigations 2)

Stateside Standalone

Welcome to Nowhere (Smithy and Diller)

Writing as C.K. McDonnell

The Stranger Times (The Stranger Times 1)

This Charming Man (The Stranger Times 2)

Love Will Tear Us Apart (The Stranger Times 3)

Visit www.WhiteHairedIrishman.com to find out more.

Milton Keynes UK
Ingram Content Group UK Ltd.
UKHW022041230824
447344UK00013B/980